SHOW STOPPER!

The Bright Lights Theatre company hit Darkville at 11.28 a.m. on Friday the 6th of May. The Junker Boys hit town at the selfsame minute . . . The Bright Lights's aim in coming to Darkville was to bring joy and culture to drab, out-of-the-way lives. Whereas the Junkers came to rob the bank.

GERALDINE McCAUGHREAN has written over a hundred books for children and adults. After many years spent working for a London publisher, she now writes full-time. Her novels have won her the Whitbread, Carnegie, Guardian, UKRA, Smarties, and Blue Peter Awards. She has also written plays for the stage and radio. Among her other books for Oxford University Press are *A Little Lower than the Angels*, *A Pack of Lies*, *Forever X*, *The Stones are Hatching*, *The Kite Rider*, and *Stop the Train*.

Other books by Geraldine McCaughrean

Geraldine McCaughrean

SHOW! STOPPER!

OXFORD
UNIVERSITY PRESS

OXFORD
UNIVERSITY PRESS

Great Clarendon Street, Oxford OX2 6DP

Oxford University Press is a department of the University of Oxford.
It furthers the University's objective of excellence in research, scholarship,
and education by publishing worldwide in

Oxford New York

Auckland Bangkok Buenos Aires
Cape Town Chennai Dar es Salaam Delhi Hong Kong Istanbul
Karachi Kolkata Kuala Lumpur Madrid Melbourne Mexico City Mumbai
Nairobi São Paulo Shanghai Taipei Tokyo Toronto

Oxford is a registered trade mark of Oxford University Press
in the UK and in certain other countries

British Library Cataloguing in Publication Data available

ISBN 0 19 275303 7

1 3 5 7 9 10 8 6 4 2

Text designed by Mike Brain Graphic Design Limited, Oxford

Printed in Great Britain
by Cox & Wyman Ltd, Reading, Berkshire

FOR FLOW

Chapter One
Bright Lights in Dark Places

The Bright Lights hit Darkville at 11.28 a.m. on Friday the 6th of May.

The Junker Boys hit town at the selfsame minute.

This is not really such a coincidence: they both arrived on the same train. But the Bright Lights Theatre Company would like it known that, apart from that time spent in adjacent carriages, hooked together by oily couplings, they have no connection whatsoever with the Junkers. The Bright Lights's aim in coming to Darkville was to bring joy and culture to drab, out-of-the-way lives.

Whereas the Junkers came to rob the bank.

Young Cissy and Kookie arrived a little later, on an up-line train, tired and sweaty and anxious. The journey had looked so short on the classroom map, and it had seemed such a good idea. Now Cissy stood in the steam-filled doorway of the carriage and said, 'I think we died on the train, Kookie, and it brought us to Hell.'

A week before, a newsy letter had arrived at the schoolhouse from their one-time teacher, Miss Loucien. Cissy had been chosen to read it out loud:

Deer Class 3

(tho I qess you may be Class 4 by now!) Sorry I aint ritten lately but I been getting Cleopatra by hart and it aint eesy. That dame sure cood tork. We bin givin it out in Nebraska and Montana and deerest Everett has been sweet like you cant emagin. IF I forget some words on stage he steers rite around me and no body is enny the whyser. Recken Shakespeer himself woodent notiss. He even rote me a song or 2 to slip in if the fokes out frunt are gettin restiv.

I miss you all sumthing feers. Just wish you cood see me in my Qeen of the Nyle getup. Nex stop The Shakespeare Theatre, Darkville—not so very far away from my favrit children in the werld. Recken if you all showted in Olive Town, Id heer you in Darkville!   Deerest Everett sends his love and so do I.

Your affecshunate friend and teecher
Loucien Crew (mrs)

To the dismay of their current teacher, Class Three immediately began to drum their feet and bang desk lids and shout, 'Haloooo, Miss Loucien!!' at the top of their voices. Miss May March rapped on her desk with a ruler, but stood no chance of quelling the riot. The summer vacation was about to start and Class Three had caught the sweet scent of Liberty. Besides, their loyalty was still to Miss May's predecessor, the glamorous Loucien Crew. Kookie Warboys had got up and rushed to the map to pinpoint Darkville: it seemed no more than a pinch of air away; a web of black railway lines wriggled clear across the space between. Surely it would be the work of moments to climb on a train and visit Miss Loucien in Darkville!

Now, two days and five connections later, Kookie and Cissy got down from the train. 'This here can't be Hell,' said Kookie reassuringly. 'We got return tickets.' But he closed his fingers tight round the precious scrap of cardboard in his pocket. Darkville certainly bore a passing resemblance to the Infernal Regions.

Darkville was a 'company town', owned by a single man. He owned the houses and he owned the mines over which Darkville was built. He owned the shops, the forge, and the fuel, the stables, the church, the saloon, and the bank. Men had to pay him good money before they could work there, trade there, live there, or even die there. In return he paid them for their labour or each crate of ore they hacked out of the ground.

As a result of the mining, high, hunched, grassless

slagheaps encircled the town, like coyotes round a carcass. There was a never-ending racket and roar of machinery and shunting trucks, conveyor belts and rock-crushers. The ground shook with subterranean rumblings, and smuts of ash swarmed through the air like a billion blowflies.

'I don't like it. I don't like this place,' said Cissy, stepping back on to the footplate of the train.

But Kookie coaxed her down. 'We come here to see Miss Loucien, not take in the sights. An' it must be civilized if they got theatre.'

'Don't look like a place they'd welcome Shakespeare,' Cissy ventured.

'Must be, if they named the theatre after him,' said Kookie, and she brightened a little. Kookie was right, as usual.

When they reached the centre of town, their spirits soared. For the Owner of Darkville had spared no expense here. Determined that not one cent of his workers' earnings should ever leave town, he had built a haven of glamour and temptation at its heart that encouraged men to squander their hard-earned cash. Gaudy, gilded three- and four-storey buildings rose up around a central plaza, announcing themselves in letters a yard high: Plaza Hotel, *The Calliope Palais*, **Universal Emporium**, The Slaked Snake Saloon, *The Ritz Dance Hall.* Wrought iron balconies glinted red in the light from wall-mounted gas-lamps. Muslin curtains blew out of the upper windows. And there, in the corner of the square—only slightly less grand than the marbled **First Darkville Bank** next door—towered the magnificent IMPERIAL SHAKESPEARE THEATRE.

Four young men not much older than Kookie and all with the same straw-blond hair, stood gazing up at the bank's marble façade, their mouths ajar.

'Nifty, huh?' said Kookie thinking to strike up conversation. He adopted the suave, man-of-the-world stance he had been practising in the schoolyard. 'Our friends are playing that theatre, don't you know?'

'So? What's that to us? We're *miners*,' said one of the young men belligerently, dragging the flap of his canvas haversack down over the sticks of dynamite inside it. '*Miners*,' he said again. 'This is a *mining* town, ain't it?'

Kookie backed off, dented a little, like a beetle that's been stepped on.

Then all of a sudden the incident was forgotten as a window opened high in the lacquered façade of the Shakespeare Theatre and a head of red hair emerged:

'*Cissy Sissney! Habakkuk Warboys! What in the name of sweet Saint George Washington do you think you're doing here?!*'

Miss Loucien clutched their heads to her bosom, looked them over as if they were a couple of cream pies . . . and then told them off roundly for coming. 'I don't know what your mothers were thinking of, letting you loose on the railroads on your own. Lord knows what dubious types you mighta run up against! That new teacher of yours ain't knocked too much sense into you yet, I see!'

She was happy. Happiness was written all over her. It was odd and slightly unsettling to see a grown-up giving off happiness like a hive gives off bees. Frontier mothers tended to leave the job of Happiness to their children, along with the other chores like chopping wood. Frontier women had too little time and energy to squander it on smiling. But Miss Loucien was plainly as happy as a dog in a butcher's pantry. Fortunately she held Cissy and Kookie partly responsible for her happiness, since it was in their town she had met the loves of her entire life: Everett Crew and the Bright Lights Theatre Company. 'Ain't this Darkville a puzzle? Looks like Trash-Can Alley and yet here's this place in the middle of it: all-glory-laud-and-honour to Mr Shakespeare. Everett says it proves good taste ain't the preserve of the wealthy.' She spoke of her husband's opinion as if she were quoting from the Bible.

Suddenly the door of her dressing room opened and a tall figure, caped and cowled, moved sideways into the room, hampered by bulky robes. He wore a white beard almost to his feet and a cloak covered in cabalistic signs. '*Prospero*,' he said, in answer to their stares. 'We're giving them *The Tempest* presently. Tell me, were we expecting to be graced with your company? Did a letter go astray? Did we know you were coming?'

Cissy trembled. Even Kookie, who was not generally at a loss for words, was silenced by the imposing bulk and camphorous smell of the wizard towering over him. They were in the way: of course they were! They had arrived uninvited! They were a couple of nuisance children! They ought not to have come.

'Nope, darlin', it was their surprise!' said Miss Loucien jumping up and kissing the wizard on the ear.

'They've come here on a whim to pay us a visit! How's that for neighbourly?'

'Ah well, then. I am greatly obliged to them,' said Everett Crew throwing back the hood of his robe and shaking them both by the hand. 'It is a great honour you've done us. A very great kindness!'

A warm glow of pride kindled within Cissy. She could not remember ever having done someone a kindness just by arriving.

'So long as they don't want paying, I don't see why they shouldn't play the "spirits descending" in tonight's show,' Everett suggested to his wife who thought it a wonderful idea.

'Us!?'

'Well, we generally use wood cut-outs but I'm sure the audience would appreciate the genuine article.'

And so Cissy and Kookie tumbled into *The Tempest* as into a property basket, barged by pieces of scenery, tripping over ropes, meeting Millie and Finn and Curly and Revere and Egil. They scuffed out chalk marks, knocked over props, ventured out onto the sloping stage and gazed out on the auditorium. 'Holy Mikey, it's big!' breathed Kookie.

Six tiers of opera-boxes rose up either wall, like carved and gilded pigeon lofts. Each had a tiny window just wide enough to allow one head to poke out. The domed ceiling was adorned with flying cupids all co-operating to hoist up a crystal chandelier, and the first and second circles were swagged with golden grapes and Tudor roses and naked nymphs.

'Ain't this the swellest place you ever saw?'

Cissy could not answer. The thought of acting in this palatial theatre, in front of an audience of hundreds, was sitting in her throat like a mouthful of scalding rabbit stew.

'This? This is nothing, son,' said Cyril Crew, passing across the stage with a bundle of costumes. 'In Denver we played the Opera House. All white and pink rococo, and *hot water in the dressing rooms*. Picture that, if you will!'

'In Olive you played in our social hall,' said Cissy. She was ashamed now that her town had been so hillbilly ramshackle in comparison with this.

'Ah, but it is the people out *there* who matter,' said the actor-manager with a grandiose sweep of one arm towards the red plush seats.

The gesture made him drop some of the costumes he was carrying and he cursed under his breath. Despite his languorous charm, Cyril Crew was not so entirely happy with life. The Owner of Darkville was demanding $50 a night for the use of his theatre. Every seat would have to be sold before Bright Lights turned a profit on the evening. A sixth sense was also niggling away at him, making him uneasy. It had something to do with the unexpected squalor of the town. It just did not seem the kind of place to value the plays of Shakespeare. There again, why else would they build a theatre in his honour? And then there was the huge number of sequins glistening in between the planks of the stage . . . What should they be telling him? he wondered. 'Make sure the trap's working, will you, Finn?' he called to a young man in the wings. 'And give some handbills to our young friends here. They can paste them up around town. We need a full house tonight.'

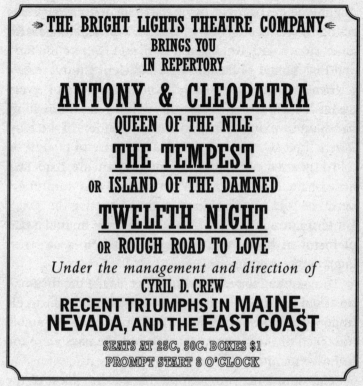

some handbills to our young friends here. They can paste them up around town. We need a full house tonight.'

Kookie went at Darkville like a man wallpapering his parlour. He stuck handbills on carts and doors, gas lamps, fences, and shop-signs. Cissy lingered longer over the work, her hand growing black from smoothing out the cheap, damp paper, her thoughts straying into daydreams.

One day she would be an actress herself. Her name would appear on handbills. She would roam the United States with the Bright Lights Company, glide into their glorious lime-lit world and receive the applause of ladies in fur wraps and gentlemen in tuxedos. Of course, she might well die of fright having actually to *go on stage and act*, but it would be worth it, almost. To have shared such an existence with Kookie and Cyril and Everett and Finn and Revere and Millie and Miss Loucien and the rest!

'Here! You gotta come along!' Kookie was urging every passer-by, thrusting rolled-up posters into unwilling hands and waxing wordy about the wonders of the play. 'There'll be swords and spears and plenty of blood!' he told a gnarled old miner swaying down the road in a haze of methylated spirits. 'Better than this dumbshow here!' he told a gang of louts queuing outside the Magic Lantern Lounge. 'Cheap at half the price!' he told a pair of Irishmen trying to string each other up to a street lamp by their braces.

'You coming to see the wondrous play at the theatre?' he asked the four blond young men crouching furtively under the bank's fire escape. He tried to push a handbill into each of their canvas satchels but the bags were too full of dynamite.

'Git, 'fore I slit your throat!' hissed the oldest of the Junker Boys, kicking Kookie in the stomach, sending him sprawling into the roadway.

Cissy expressed the opinion—as she hauled Kookie to his feet, looped his arm around her neck and helped him back on to the plaza—that the people of Darkville were a touch in need of 'cultivating'.

Chapter Two
The House that Jack Built

Miss Loucien applied powder to their upturned faces as if she were putting talcum on twin babies. She checked the ropes knotted around their chests and called, 'Haul away!' And Attendant Spirit One and Attendant Spirit Two rose slowly into the flies above the stage. A dozen mothballs spilled from the pocket of Cissy's costume and rattled down on the stage like acorns. She and Kookie climbed astride the broadest beam and settled down to watch the play unfold below them. Cyril warned them they might have a two-hour wait before their entrance and on no account to fall asleep as he did not want attendant spirits 'crashing to earth like d****d albatrosses in the middle of Act One.'

'Don't mind him,' Miss Loucien had said. 'He's a perfectionist.'

'How will we know when our part comes?' whispered Cissy now, wide-eyed with fright.

''Spect Finn will give us a tug on the ropes,' said Kookie, nonchalant as can be. For a fleeting moment, Cissy wanted to push him off his beam. How could he stay so cool in the face of this appalling ordeal? She wished her pa were sitting out front in the audience. She thanked her stars that her mother was not. She wished she were home in her hammock, reading the journals that draught-proofed the walls of her bedroom. She wished herself anywhere but here, squeezed into a dress made from lace curtains, waiting to play her debut role.

The street doors were opened. The great red curtains were drawn closed. Beyond them, invisible, the audience began to arrive. Heavy work boots could be heard thudding up the aisles; also the click-clack of the doors into the boxes. A strange, sour smell began to rise off the rose-red auditorium—a smell of tobacco and wet socks and sweat and used whisky. An usher in the maroon livery of the theatre called in a droning voice for 'all liquor bottles to be left outside . . . all liquor bottles to be left outside, all liquor bottles to be le— *ouch!*' and fell suddenly silent.

From their high roost the children could see into the wings. They saw the Crew brothers exchange puzzled frowns. The cast drifted in from their dressing rooms to peer through chinks in the curtain. None of them seemed to like what they saw—though to Kookie and Cissy it sounded like a frighteningly full house. But three strangers had joined the Crew brothers in the wings, and a heated argument was starting up.

'Fifty dollars. Cash,' said the Owner of Darkville. He was dressed in a smoking jacket, Turkish cap, and army boots and sucked on a Russian cigarette as long and black as a liquorice stick.

'That is understood, sir, and I shall bring it round to you, in person, directly after the play. Out-of-the-takings.'

'Now. Payment up front. That's how it works here. In this town people pay me *before* they dig. Saves disappointment. And broken teeth.' Two prodigious men the shape of beer kegs stepped up to the Owner's shoulder.

'Psst! Kookie! Mr Cyril is gettin' strong-armed!' Cissy whispered, but Kookie had already seen. He pointed out the large army pistols worn over each man's belly.

Suddenly Curly, the Company's little bald bookkeeper, joined the growing crowd in the wings. He was clutching a handkerchief to his nose. 'Mr Cyril, sir! Mr Cyril! They won't pay! Not one! Just push their way in! In numbers, sir! In numbers! Ticketless! I can get no remedy against this consumption of the purse! The rumpus in the foyer, sir! You should see it! Chaos is come again!' Queasy at the sight of blood—especially his own—Curly took the handkerchief away from his nose and sagged at the knees.

'How am I expected to pay if the audience won't pay me?' asked Cyril, all injured outrage.

'Oh, they'll pay . . . if they see anything they like.'

Cyril was having to shout now, to make himself heard above the noise in the auditorium. 'In that case, I believe, sir, that I shall decline your colourful hospitality and go!' and he began to take off his Tudor doublet.

'You do that,' snarled the Owner. 'You can pay the $50 on your way out. Theatre's booked and you took the booking. You want my boys here should shake it outa you?'

To give him his due, Cyril did not reach instantly for his wallet. (Perhaps he knew it did not contain $50.)

'Kindly let us maintain a level of civilized dialogue here, Mr . . . Mr . . . '

'Shakespeare,' snarled the Owner, pushing a haystack of snuff up the kinked passageways of his nose. 'Jack Shakespeare.'

'Ah.'

That was when everyone's unformed fears were realized. That was when all their dark suspicions came home to roost, like crows to an elm tree.

'So, Mr . . . ah . . . Shakespeare, you are the man after whom this theatre is . . . '

'. . . named, yeah, yeah. You think I'm gonna call it after my mother, maybe?'

'Ah,' said Cyril again. 'In that case, Mr . . . ah . . . may I call you Jack? I believe my colleagues and I *may* have come here under a certain . . . *misapprehension*.' His smile was apologetic, his colour draining to milk-white.

Jack Shakespeare bared his teeth too, but not in a smile. 'Listen, molly. I don't care if you come here under a hot-air balloon. *Gimme the fifty bucks or my boys are gonna break your nancy legs for you!*'

Every member of the cast had to search their pockets before the full fifty dollars could be mustered. As the Owner rammed the money into his quilted silk pockets, he cast one last look of contempt over Cyril's Elizabethan costume, spat, and left, snarling, 'Word of advice. Better give these saps what they want, molly, or they'll take you limb from limb. Any damage to my theatre and you'll pay for that too.'

All this while, the rose-red auditorium had been filling up, the customers growing restless. Threatened by a man wielding an empty bottle, the liveried usher ran to the curtain pulls and—ready or not—the scarlet velvet gave a jerking twitch. Up in the flies, Kookie prised Cissy's fingers out of her ears and broke the news to her that the curtains were opening. The show—ready or not—was about to begin.

The sight that met those on either side of the curtains was a shock to everyone. The audience, who weekly assembled to watch can-can girls and chanteuses, contortionists and conjurors, were confronted by two oddly clad men clutching a ship's prow and shouting:

'Fall to't yarely or we run ourselves aground: bestir, bestir!'

'Hey, my hearts! Cheerly, cheerly, my hearts! Yare, yare! Take in the topsail!'

The actors, for their part, looked out on a fully lit auditorium crammed with sprawling, smoking, eating, drinking, coughing, spitting miners lying across three and four seats. Boys were selling tobacco, sweets, and pistachio nuts out of peddler-trays. Dogs chased each other in and out of the legs of latecomers and bar-boys fetching in pint glasses from the Slaked Snake Saloon. Two men were arm-wrestling in the second row and several card games were in progress. There were no women—not a one—unless you counted the girls leaning against the wall, who seemed to have forgotten their dresses and come out in only their corsets and drawers.

'Hence! What cares these roarers for the name of king? To cabin! Silence! Trouble us not!'

For one hundred sweet seconds the audience sat or stood and stared, stock-still, unnerved by the stage lightning flickering on and off. Darkville had never seen a shipwreck depicted on stage before. In fact it had never seen drama of any kind (unless it was that night Conchita Vargas shot her lover in the head).

Then the scene changed to 'Prospero's island cell' and Everett recklessly let rip with a dozen 300-year-old lines of Shakespearean verse.

Now, the Bright Lights were all accustomed to pitching their plays at different kinds of audience. In the backwoods they tended to perform melodrama or farce. But the actors had been so taken in by the theatre's name that they had prepared nothing simpler. Only Shakespeare.

'What language is he speaking?' someone asked his neighbour.

'Give us some magic, if you're going to!' shouted someone else, from the circle, thinking Prospero's robes were part of a magic act.

'When she's gonna sing?' another wanted to know, pointing at Millie who was the only other person on stage.

After five or eight more lines of *The Tempest*, a genuinely bewildered young man rose to his feet in the stalls and asked, 'What's a-doing here?'

And Everett Crew unwisely stepped up to the footlights and said, 'Well, gentlemen . . . Shakespeare!'

If there had ever been a chance of salvaging the evening, it died with that one word: *Shakespeare*. The tyrannical Owner of Darkville was so hated by his workforce that the mere mention of his name soured their whole mood.

Cyril still stood in the wings, paralysed with indecision. Everett, reading the danger signs, took the decision to abandon the play. He stepped off the stage— took one long stride over thin air on to the top of an upright piano then hopped down on to the seat, intending to bang out a song. It might just save the situation. But when he threw open the lid and began to play he thought he must have gone deaf, for no notes sounded at all.

The miners behind him hooted with laughter. 'Frankie Muldoon used the wire for sieving his slack!' they roared, and when Everett flipped up the top lid, he found the piano was indeed as hollow as a drum. 'Never fear,' the men added. 'We hanged him fer doin' it.'

So Millie began to sing the only unaccompanied song she could call to mind—the Willow Song from *Othello*. Given her lack of practice, she made a truly dismal job of it.

'O willow, willow, willow, willow, shall be my garland!
O willow, willow, willow, willow . . .'

She was as flat as Holland.

'Oh, Lor'. We're gonna get killed,' said Kookie to Cissy, up in the flies.

Soon two hundred jeering miners were howling out the refrain: 'Owwwww! Willow, willow, willow, willow, willow, *willowwowoow!*' like demented wolves baying for blood. Someone threw the remains of the loaf he was eating. Then the arm snapped off a seat, and that was thrown, too.

'Hold thy peace! I prithee hold thy peace!' sang Everett in his rich Shakespearean baritone. (Well, someone had to mount a rescue mission to save Millie.)

Revere took the hint and ran on stage: *'Hold thy peace, I prithee hold thy peace!'*

It was a round; there needed to be three of them to sing it. Everett beckoned his brother to come out of the wings, but Cyril was still staring, dazed, into the middle distance. So Everett and Revere cajoled the house into three sections and got everybody singing. It held them in their seats for about as long as straw bales keep cattle penned in.

Egil could do some juggling.

Finn recited 'The Boy Stood on the Burning Deck'.

But the miners out front had been expecting high-stepping floozies wearing feathers and sequins; they began to chant—*'More skin! More skin!'*—and bang their gigantic boots and slam the empty seats up and down. *'More skin! More skin! More skin!'*

'Do something! Can you do anything? I can only do cartwheels!' Kookie hissed at Cissy.

'I can only stand on my head,' sobbed Cissy, a world of apology in her voice. If only she could spin from a trapeze by her teeth or saw a horse in half or perform the Indian Rope Trick or dive one thousand feet into a glass of milk!

Then—after the shrillest of ear-splitting whistles—a sight of such extraordinary power and majesty emerged through the back curtain that cast and audience alike fell silent: the Queen of the Nile, complete with cobra crown, asp, and bullwhip. She was wearing a gold breastplate and diaphanous skirt, scarab amulet, train whistle, and pointed sandals. With her long red hair hanging loose to her waist, Miss Loucien looked less like Cleopatra than Boudicca the night she burned Colchester. When she proceeded to take out the footlights one by one with cracks of the bullwhip, it seemed not a soul was breathing in the whole of Darkville. Even the click of gamblers' dice ceased in the opera boxes, and heads poked out to watch, poppy-eyed. Cleopatra sent fourteen tin lampshades spinning into the auditorium.

'O, my Egypt!' said Everett under his breath. Unlike Cissy and Kookie (who had studied whip-cracking as one of Miss Loucien's unique and varied school lessons), he had never seen this aspect of his magnificent wife.

The miners whistled. The miners threw screwed up paper money. The miners stood on their seats and held up their hats for Loucien to cull with a lick of rawhide and a noise like a pistol shot.

She was a triumph—until, that is, one over-enthusiastic admirer grabbed the tail of the whip and pulled it out of her hand. Cleopatra would have to fall back on some other accomplishment.

'Tell them a story!' Cissy called down in her tiniest voice. She recalled happy hours spent under the schoolyard tree listening to Choctaw legends. But Kookie had suddenly recalled another memory of his schooldays. Ruching up his Attendant Spirit costume, despite his awkward position on the narrow beam, he reached two fingers into his jeans pocket. In a moment, the sweet quacking strains of his harmonica cut through the drunken roar of the Friday-night revellers.

When lesser teachers might have been wasting children's time on writing or maths, Miss Loucien was teaching them 'Soapsuds over the Fence' and 'Shenandoah' and more. Now Kookie played 'My Love is a Rider', while on stage the company of actors assembled, crooning, harmonizing or la-la-ing, according to how well they knew the song.

It was a rousing song, a patriotic song, a song with enough religion in it to remind the men of their Sunday School days when their manners had been a lot better. Being full of whisky by now, the audience began to leak at the eyes. Two of the dogs joined in, howling.

And the night might have been saved—but for that drunken troublemaker in the third row. Armed now with the bullwhip, he lurched forward like a sleepy salamander uncoiling its tongue, and flicked the lash around Loucien's waist, aiming to drag her off the stage and into his arms.

Everett, after twenty minutes of heroic and exhausting effort, had to endure seeing his wife dragged painfully over the remains of the footlights and embraced by a drunken hooligan. All calm and coolness deserted him. Hurling himself off the stage, he landed on the lout with the whip and wrestled him to the floor. Loucien struggled back over the footlights, like a swimmer dragged aboard a rescue boat. Finn and Egil urged her and Millie to 'get off stage and hide', but she was loath to leave Everett to the mercy of the mob.

A noise like monstrous hailstones signalled that the miners had begun throwing all the small change from their pockets. Coins thrown hard and from a great height make lethal missiles. Dimes ricocheted around the stage, hitting backs turned and arms raised in self-defence. Revere was hit in the back of the skull and fell to his knees. Cyril bled from a cut under one eye. The whole sea of grimy spectators began to surge towards the stage, like a riptide threatening to engulf a beach.

'On the count of three . . . run for your lives,' Cyril instructed his cast, through a sea fret of flying cents and nickels. 'One . . . two . . .'

But he never reached three.

With a shock wave, then an ear-shattering bang, a massive explosion shook the Imperial Shakespeare Theatre. The trapdoor in the centre of the stage blew out and spun so high in the air that it struck Kookie's dangling boot.

The pelmet of the proscenium arch collapsed and twin tongues of scarlet velvet licked outwards into the auditorium. The actors were knocked off their feet; the miners (well acquainted with explosions) curled up in the aisles, with their hats over their faces and their arms over their heads.

The glass chandelier, its nerve finally shattered, came crashing down like the coming of the Seventh Ice Age.

Then the rear doors flew open and someone yelled, 'The bank! They've blown up the bank!'

Chapter Three
A Price to Pay

'What was *that*?' said Revere stumbling to his feet.

'That was Salvation wearing a stick of dynamite in its hatband,' said Everett. 'For a minute there I thought we were in difficulties.' He and his wife touched hands. There are times when being in love makes life more alarming rather than less. 'Though I never thought to say it: here's to crime!' Sitting down on the edge of the stage, he looked for once as old as his brother, the lines of his face exaggerated by weariness and spirit gum. He rolled his false beard into a cotton boll and threw it aside.

Millie emerged from behind the curtain, coughing, as dust from the explosion continued to settle. Curly joined them, still dabbing at his bloody nose. ''Twas caviar to the general,' he said, bemoaning the audience's lack of enthusiasm for Shakespeare.

They looked out across a deserted auditorium strewn with hats and bottles and playing cards. They covered and uncovered their ears experimentally, finding the explosion had left them all a little deaf.

'Gather up the cash, and let's get out of here, for God's sake,' said Cyril, 'before that b***d in the dressing gown comes back asking for damages.'

'*Ahmm*. Can we come down now, please?' called Kookie.

'Lor'! The hero of the mouth-organ!' cried Miss Loucien tipping her head back to peer into the roof. 'What would your mothers say if they could see you now?—No, don' tell me! Your mother, Habakkuk, would make everyone a cup of mint tea and a mustard poultice. And yours, Cissy, would sweep us all to Tallahassee with a twig broom!'

Kookie and Cissy laughed, but they felt saggy and heavy limbed and a little sick thinking what might have happened. It was almost as if the explosion had thrown them up into the roof and wedged them among the rafters. Revere went to the rope wound figure-of-eight-style around a hook in the wall and lowered Cissy down.

'Out of this nettle, danger, we pluck this flower, safety,' Curly greeted her. (The bookkeeper found more uses for Shakespeare's words than all the actors put together.)

Revere was just about to fetch Kookie down as well, when the double doors were again thrown open at the back of the auditorium. Already damaged, the hinges on one gave way and the door fell askew. During the brief moment it took those outside to kick the door aside, Loucien stepped smartly in front of Cissy, hiding her from sight. She also shot Revere a look that stopped him lowering Kookie out of the flies.

Clambering past the fallen door, trampling the litter

23

and broken glass in the aisles, the miners of Darkville came streaming back into the auditorium, their faces smutted with soot, their teeth showing white through beards of grime. The actors on the stage instinctively got to their feet and moved closer together, like livestock sensing slaughter.

The mob was led by a man in railway uniform, who pointed at the stage with the railway cap rolled up in his hands. 'I tell you they come in on the same train! Saw them with my own eyes! Diversion they were! Keep us busy while their cronies blew the bank!'

'. . . in it together.'

'. . . it together.'

'. . . together.' The words passed backwards through the mob like sweets handed out among children.

'They were packing up to go! See?'

Loucien reached behind her and took hold of Cissy's dress, gripping so hard that the lace tore and laddered with a pop-popping noise. Cissy was clenched so close up against Miss Loucien's back that she could see the sweat trickling down it. The heels of the Egyptian sandals came to rest on Cissy's toes but she did not cry out. Suddenly Miss Loucien stepped forwards—striding right across the gaping open trap in the centre of the stage and dropping Cissy through it into the gloomy, choking space beneath.

Cissy knew better than to struggle. She stayed as she fell, curled up on hands and knees. Dust and smoke and the smell of cordite and charred wood invaded her nose and throat and would have made her eyes water if they had not been already full of tears. If she screwed her head right round, she could see Kookie's face looking down at her from high above the stage—like a kingfisher watching a fish in a brook. They fixed their eyes on one another, as if to look away would allow disaster to sweep everything away forever.

Cyril Crew was trying to calm the situation. 'What seems to be the—' There was the noise of someone cocking a pistol.

'You're in league with them, the whole pack of you!'

'Let's string 'em up!'

'No! They can say where the money's gone!'

Like flotsam beached by the sea, the miners crowded up against the stage—a crush of angry, vengeful drunks. Next door, their town bank had been reduced to a hollow ruin—a cave of lathe and plaster, peppered with dimes and nickels like so many rabbit droppings. The great safe, which had held secure their hard-earned savings, lay on its back as useless as a coffin on the Day of Resurrection.

'I had $400 saved up for a house in Nebraska!'

'Another month and I coulda been outa here!'

'Ten years! For what? Ten years hard labour I put in, for what? Nothing!'

Marriages and journeys, businesses and retirements, dreams and ambitions had all been blasted to extinction by the raid on the Darkville Company Bank. These men had laboured in Hell while each saved up for his private idea of Heaven. Now they wanted recompense, even if it was only in blood.

A trio of ash-blond youths had been seen riding out of town at the gallop on stolen horses, their clothes in rags around them, trailing a charred smell suited to three such devils. But that blond hair had drawn attention to them—not just as they escaped but earlier, at the station, when they had disembarked . . . alongside the actors and luggage of the Bright Lights Theatre Company.

Now the platform guard was giving his testimony, and a jury of two hundred angry men were leaping to quite the wrong conclusion.

'We saw 'em! We saw them three with the yeller hair! Your conspirators! The ones yer in league with! Where they gone, eh? Which way they heading? Tell us, 'fore we beat it outa you!'

Cyril Crew was noisy in his protestations of innocence. ' . . . A mere accident of timing! Travelling in adjacent carriages is hardly . . . no call for this hasty . . .'

But his brother was silent.

Everett Crew—whose power of oratory had held whole towns in thrall—whose mouth had held the words of Caesar and Chatterton, of Byron and the Bible, of Webster and Washington—was wholly wordless now. His thoughts were for his wife. Could he have plunged her any deeper into danger, he wondered, if they had honeymooned among the alligators of the Everglades or the scalping Comanche of the Black Hills? Without glancing upwards he was aware of the red-haired boy in the rafters above him, the girl hastily hidden beneath his feet. What would become of them, after everyone else on stage had been dragged away, tried summarily, and lynched by the miners of Darkville? No, Everett Crew could see that things had gone much too far for words to put right. And so he said nothing—though one line of

26

Shakespeare kept spinning, spinning, spinning through his brain like one of those angry, flying coins: *The bright day is done, And we are for the dark.*

He shook his head. His long, dishevelled hair shed chalk-dust, making it appear that his soul was somehow in the process of stealing out of his body.

As the actors were dragged outside, the emptying theatre fell silent.

Worming his way along the beam, Kookie tried to work out how to get down. With his safety rope still wound round its hook, he could happily jump off the beam and still be left dangling twenty feet up in the air. If he took off the rope harness, he could equally get down from the beam very fast indeed—and not nearly so happily. Twenty feet is a long way to fall.

'Cissy! Pssst! You gonna have to lower me down!'

Ever so slowly Cissy's head emerged through the trap in the centre of the stage. Eyes wide, she looked around her for any sign of the actors or the lynch mob. But the theatre was empty once more and so quiet that she could hear the sighing hiss of the gas-lamps still flickering amid their shattered glass mantles.

'Help me down!' Kookie whispered insistently. 'I'm no good to anyone up here!'

'What's going to happen, Kookie?' Dazed and clumsy she fumbled with the rope as if she had never seen rope before.

'We're gonna save the day, that's what!'

'How?'

'Don't know yet but it'll come to me. Just lower me down.'

'Cain't,' said Cissy dully.

'Why not? It's just like lowering a washline!'

'But you weigh ten times more 'n the washing!' And with those skinny arms clenched against her ribs, as thin and white as pipe-cleaners, it was true Cissy looked hardly strong enough to fetch in washing. Her grimy face kept swivelling towards the trap or the wrecked rear doors of the theatre, as she yearned after Miss Loucien and the rest. She should never have let them be taken without saying a word! She should never have crouched there, still and silent, while Miss Loucien and the Bright Lights were dragged off to the nearest hanging tree . . . ! And yet what could she have done? She hadn't even the strength to haul down Attendant Spirit One out of the flies!

Instead, she made a loop in the rope, slipped her foot into the loop, then unwound the contents of the figure-of-eight hook. Shutting her eyes, she said, 'Git off now!'

Doubtfully, Kookie eased one cautious leg over the beam—got the heel of his boot caught in a lacy hem, and lost his balance. He came off the beam with a squawk, his harness round his hips, and he descended towards the floor like a sack of sugar. Cissy the Counterweight, on the other hand, rose gracefully into the air, clutching the rope close against her cheek, keeping her eyes so tightly shut that coloured lights flickered within her lids.

Kookie came to rest with his nose a few inches off the

floor, his costume popping every seam, hands and feet flailing.—'Wonderful! Now I'm down and you're up!'—But somehow, via sheer bravado and several rope burns, Kookie did manage to lower Cissy down in one piece.

'They really think Mr Cyril's a bank robber,' she said as she descended. She was like someone in a dream.

'A 'complice, anyway,' said Kookie. 'That's not so bad.'

'But if they still hang 'complices . . . ?' Cissy could not see that the distinction mattered very much.

'Yes. But it's not as bad a crime to be hanged for, is what I meant.' With the toe of his boot Kookie pushed at the square of wood that had been blown out of the stage by the explosion. 'Did you see that bang? Did you see how the trapdoor went up! *Peeeow!* How'd it do that?'

'The bang came clear through from the bank next door,' said Cissy. 'It's all bricks and splinters down there. Taste of gunpowder, strong as baking soda!'

Kookie was still remembering. '*Peeeow!* Came clear up and hit my boot. Thought it was gonna knock us off! Thought for a minute someone had up and thrown a stick of dynamite cos they hated the play! *We ain't that bad*, I thought!'

At the mention of dynamite, he interrupted himself. His thoughts drifted back to earlier in the day—to the boys with the haversacks, loitering outside the bank—*'This is a mining town, ain't it? We're miners.'* 'We saw them!' he said, with a gasp. 'We actually 'changed words with the bank robbers! Recall? Bunch of palomino blonds? Wouldn't take a playbill off us?'

'There were four,' said Cissy.

'Mmm. Three or four.'

Cissy grabbed her friend by both cuffs and wagged his hands violently up and down. 'Don't you hear what I'm saying? There were *four*! That miner said just now, three had ridden outa town. But there were *four*.'

Kookie cast his mind back. Four, yes, she was right. A lookout, probably, who had got away ahead of the others. Another 'complice.

But Cissy was squatting down again on the edge of the trap, posting her legs down into the dark, letting herself drop, painfully, in among the rubble and stench. 'Three got away and the fourth one didn't!' she called as she jumped.

Kookie was sceptical. 'How do you work that out?'

'That's what I've been trying to tell you, Kooks! The fourth one got blowed clear through the wall . . . And he's still down here!'

Chapter Four
The Necktie

The Junker brothers had done a lot of bad things in their lives, but bank robbery was not one of them. They had never turned their hand to it before. They knew that it involved dynamite but not how much. Consequently, they had blown apart not only the bank's safe but also its vault, its desks, its booths, its water jugs and crockery, its portraits of the Owner and the President, and the telegraph machine. They had blown the clothes off their backs and the eyebrows off their faces. The youngest—Billy Junker—had been thrown twenty feet through a collapsing wall, into the theatre basement next door.

In fact he lay so buried in rubble that Cissy was afraid at first she had found only his head. He had covered his face when the fuse was lit, and now two ghostly hand-shapes were traced in white on his blast-blackened face. His white-blond hair, almost luminous in the dark, lifted in the draught, but he lay so still that Kookie and Cissy thought he must be dead. Then he gave a whimper. 'Tom? Haddy? Where are yuh? Josh?'

'I'll go fetch help,' said Cissy. But of course she could

not. The only help the men of Darkville would bring Billy Junker was a heave-ho to Hell. '*Do* something, Kookie! Your ma stitches up everybody back home! She musta taught you something!'

Kookie gave a convulsive shudder. He would not admit as much to Cissy, but he hated the sight of blood. Even now he was fearful of what he might see if there was more light to see by. Instead he said, 'What'ya wanna help him for? He's a bank robber! They're gonna hang Miss Loucien cos of him . . . Knew you were no good, soon as I saw you in the square.'

But Cissy simply began lifting away the rubble: chunks of brick, clods of earth, sticks of furniture, a cash-box . . . It was like doing a jigsaw: gradually the thin, ragged shape of Bill Junker emerged. 'The town people think our friends were in league with you,' she explained to him as she worked. 'The actors, you know? Our friends? You could tell them it wasn't so. Elsewise they're gonna lynch . . .' She broke off, too full of horror to say the words.

Kookie gave a snort of disgust. 'No use telling him. A lot he cares! People like him. We're just saps and stooges. People like him.'

Cissy reached out in the dark and gave Kookie such a shove that he rolled over backwards and banged his head on a brick. From somewhere beneath them came a grumbling drone, like an accordion without a keyboard or a bagpipe without a chanter. The ground below seemed to be clearing its throat to speak.

'What is this place?' asked Billy, taking in his surroundings for the first time.

'You're under a stage. The stage in a theatre. The bank's thataway.' Cissy spoke politely, as if giving directions to a stranger.

'Don't care for the dark much,' said Billy.

'You got three minutes to tell us where they're taking the money.'

Ray Coghill, a toolmaker, had appointed himself leader of the mob (though the stationmaster was eager not to be sidelined, after being the one to finger the actors).

'This is ridiculous,' Cyril continued to say whenever there was a lull in the abuse. 'We have nothing to do with all this! We don't know who you are talking about!'

'We'll hang you one by one till you talk!' squeaked Coghill.

'*Where were you planning to meet up?*'

'*Where were you gonna pick up your share?*'

'Four years I worked for that money!' a plaintive voice reminded them all. 'I say we should hang 'em anyway!'

'*Stop this.* You're scaring the women,' said Everett with a voice of such authority that those holding on to Loucien and Millie did let go.

But the posse sent after the fleeing bank robbers had returned empty-handed, and desperation was at work among the victims of the robbery: desperation and devilment.

'Times a-passing!' sneered Jack Shakespeare, overseeing matters from the balcony of the Plaza Hotel where he lived. There was a smug kind of glee about the man, a smirking relish that seemed to find amusing the fact that the actors had come under suspicion.

'Prove you don't know 'em!' demanded the stationmaster. 'Huh? Huh?'

'How can a person *prove* they *don't* know someone?' begged Millie.

'Exactly!' said the stationmaster in triumph.

Loucien Crew, still bizarrely dressed as Cleopatra, tried to restore some calm, pitching her voice low and soothing. 'Banks carry insurance. It's the bank that has to carry the loss if it's robbed. That's what banks are all about. That's why people use banks—to have their money safe, come what might!'

For a moment the mood of vengeful hysteria faltered. Men glanced towards the Owner, standing up there on his balcony pulling on his fat cigar.

'Ah well now . . . that ain't quite exact,' said Jack Shakespeare, surprisingly cheerful for a man whose bank has been robbed and half demolished. 'In the fiscal sense, Darkville Bank ain't a bank as such. It's a fy-nanshal ree-pos-i-tory.' (He pronounced it one syllable at a time, like a man hammering shut a coffin.) 'It don't make bank charges; don't make loans. Town strongbox is what it was . . . till you and your cronies busted it open. You were seen. Why deny it? You were seen with them others. Connivin'. Conspirin'. Di-ver-shun-arry tac-tics, that's what! Thought I smelled a rat when I first saw yuh!'

'But it was *you who booked us*, sir!' cried Cyril. He and his company seemed to have dropped into Hell through some conjuror's trapdoor, and now they were going to be made to disappear completely.

'Three minutes are up,' the Owner pointed out, whirling his fob watch out of his waistcoat pocket, letting it swing, noose-like, in the warm night air as a reminder that he alone in Darkville had control over Time.

The jigsaw was almost complete: Cissy had lifted aside each lump of earth and masonry to reveal the whole of Billy Junker. When the dynamite had gone off, the bank's small change must have been sent spinning outwards at the speed of bullets. That shower of cents thrown onstage by the rowdy audience had been nothing to this artillery, this buckshot, this hail of twisted nickel. The miners' small change had found its target, too—in Billy. In the dim light, his waistcoat and breeches glimmered with metal studs.

'We'll get you out of here,' said Cissy. 'Then you can tell the Owner how we had nothing to do with it!'

'Oh yeah,' said Kookie sourly. 'Great character witness, I'm sure!'

Cissy gasped with irritation. 'Look, Habakkuk Warboys, he's just a boy. People don't treat boys the same as criminals!'

Kookie snorted. 'You tell my mother that, will yuh, Cecelia Sissney? That's if we ever see home again!'

* * *

First they had trouble finding a rope, and then in remembering how to tie a noose so that it pulled up smooth and tight. Revere (who had a sailor's knowledge of knots) decided not to offer them any advice.

They laid hands on Curly first. But Cyril Crew held up a hand: 'As Player-Manager, I believe the onus should fall on me first!'

'No, no!' protested Curly. *'Men must endure Their going hence, even as their coming hither; Ripeness is all!'*

But Everett Crew put a hand on Curly's arm and said in kindly reproof, 'Very apt, Curly, but kindly observe the billing.'

'The wha'?' said the man with the noose.

'The billing, sir. In the world of Theatre, billing is everything, and I, Everett Crew, have had top billing in six states!'

A murmur of puzzlement ran through the crowd. 'Anyone'd think they was in a hurry to get their necks stretched!'

Everett swept back his hair with both hands in a gesture beloved of evangelical preachers. 'Not at all, sir, but where I come from, a good necktie speech is the zenith of a man's career!'

'What's the hold up?' called Jack Shakespeare from his balcony. 'Just get on and hang him!'

They lifted Everett up on to a big old dray horse, the noose around his neck, and flung the end up to Shakespeare, who threaded it over the balcony rail and dropped it back down. Then the Owner turned away inside—as if lynchings were an entertainment beneath his dignity.

'You got something you want to say?' said the stationmaster, feeling they were getting no closer to recovering the stolen money.

'Nothing I couldn't say better at the saloon bar with a whisky in my hand,' said Everett gamely.

There was a ripple of laughter, an appreciation of 'style'.

'Well, I sure have, if he hasn't,' said Loucien. 'I only just married the guy.' Another ripple of laughter.

'Talk, if you know what's good for you!' snarled the stationmaster.

And Everett did.

He mustered his thoughts as a cowboy musters cattle. Then he applied himself to making a necktie speech, knowing it had to last him the rest of his life.

'I was born at a very early age, and found in a racoon-tail hat, on the plains of Wichita. The wolves and coyotes were just arguing over who should eat me, when there chanced along a certain Arapaho squaw remarkable for her beauty and the prodigious length of her hair. She took me home, and her pa—the Chief, that is—was so impressed that he made up his mind to remove my innards and use me for a medicine bag. But his daughter had this quantity of hair (as I've said). No comb was equal to it, and this was proving a handicap in the marriage stakes, since her suitors feared to lose their way in that great jungle of tresses. So she swapped me at the trading post for a hairbrush and a half dozen tortoiseshell hairgrips, and I was sold on, as a job lot, in with a coal-scuttle, some pegs, and a dress-length of calico.

'Now the lady for whom this calico was intended . . .'

* * *

Cissy and Kookie cleared a path through the broken masonry and charred litter, and began dragging Billy by his feet. They set off towards the stage trap, but, once there, found there was no way the two of them could lift him. So they fetched Prospero's cloak and, laying it out alongside Billy, somehow rolled him into it. Now, perhaps, they could carry Billy outside and confront the mob with a first-hand witness to the truth.

'You really think he gives two figs for the truth?' hissed Kookie, cold with fear, and sour with disgust and contempt for Cissy's simplicity.

'He might want to ease his conscience!' she hissed back, equally angry at Kookie's cynicism. Could he not see? There was no *point* in doubting. They had no other choice.

For a scrawny young man, Billy Junker weighed tremendously heavy. It was not until they pulled off his boots that Cissy could even lift her end of the cloak. Bent double by the lowness of the stage, they heaved and dragged their 'witness' as far as the crazed floor of the bank vault. A chair still lay smouldering in a corner. Lead from the body of the safe had actually liquefied and re-set in a shiny metal puddle. It was a scene of total devastation.

Billy Junker began calling again for his brothers.

'They run off and left you, mister,' said Kookie with satisfaction. 'See what kind they are? They're probably glad you got blowed up! Only gotta share the money three ways now!'

Cissy tried to shame him with a look, but he had his eyes screwed shut with the effort of lifting.

And Billy said: 'Money? What money? The safe was empty.'

Chapter Five
The Drop

In Darkville, you see, Jack Shakespeare thought he owned more than the mines and buildings. He thought his monopoly ran to more than shops and houses, ore mills and shunt yards. He liked to think the Truth was his to alter as well; that Right and Wrong were simply the difference between what he wanted and what everyone else did.

He had sent for the Junker Boys to come and blow the Darkville Bank. He had even told them the day to come, and booked a show in at the theatre, so as to clear the streets for them. Then, the day before they were due, Shakespeare had emptied the safe himself, replacing the money with a single bag of cents and a large wrap of dynamite.

The way Jack saw it, since the miners' lives already belonged to him, their savings should, too.

'He even mailed us the keys,' said Billy with a wry smile. 'Was gonna meet up with us in Holeville and take his cut. "Money for jam," he said. Never guessed he was fixing to eat all the jam himself and leave us carrying the can.' A trickle of redness escaped Billy's mouth: Cissy feared it was not jam.

'You gonna tell them, then, Billy? Them out there? That the Owner did it? That you got nothing? That the Bright Lights had nothing to do with it?'

Billy Junker licked his lips and frowned, coughing but lacking the strength to cough. 'Lights?' he said, casting his eyes about again listlessly. 'Where? I don't care for all this dark.'

'So I took the fifth ace out of my boot and played it, and that's how I came to win the hand of my second wife,' Everett Crew was saying '—though I had to play sixteen more games to win the rest of her anatomy.'

Some of the crowd had sat down to listen. Someone had been to the saloon to fetch Crew a pint of beer as his voice was starting to break from dryness. The big horse was restless, tossing its head up and down, troubled by the smoke from the many pipes that had been lit.

'Now, the only complaint I'd make about my wedding day was the lamentable lack of presents. All we got given was a dog. But what a dog! A pure-bred mongrel puppy from a long line of champion, pedigree mongrels. And it had such a magical nose for politics that it could tell if a man was Republican or Democrat just by sniffing the inside of his hat! When news of this came to the ears of Government, I was obliged to give him up, in the cause of Life, Liberty, and the American

Way. But the President rewarded me by making me honorary senator of Newfoundland for a year and a day. Now, you may not realize this, my friends, but Newfoundland lies, like a scraping of lard, over Oldfoundland—legendary home of the Cumquats . . .'

Showers of plaster trickled down on to their heads, like the lime sprinkled into graves. At any moment, the cracks in the ceiling above their heads might gape wide and let in the night sky and all the roof timbers, too.

Gently, gently, Kookie and Cissy heaved their heavy load over the debris: the tellers' booths had all collided to form a mountain range of splintered wood and tortured metal grilles. Sometimes Kookie led the way and sometimes Cissy, their clenched fists tucked up by their chins, their backs screaming from the weight of the young man inside the cloak.

The hot glass of broken gas-lamps had fallen on to a sisal rug, climbed up the cords of the wood-slat blinds, and was now a hoop of flame encircling the door. Singly, they might have dashed through and out into the street beyond, but Billy Junker was in no fit state to dash anywhere. Cissy and Kookie stood for a moment looking at the doorbell jumping and ringing among the flames. *Coming? Coming?* it seemed to say, in tones of rising hysteria.

They laid down Billy and looked for something to douse the fire. Cissy found it in the bottom drawer of a desk—drinking water in a screw-top bottle, or so she supposed. Kookie came stumbling back with a fire bucket full of sand just in time to see Cissy throw the bottle. 'Cissy, *no! Not that! That's . . .'*

Tasting the gin, the fire splashed as high as the ceiling, setting a portrait of George Washington alight. They stood on either side of the bucket flinging fistfuls of sand at the flames, but it was like trying to stave off a ravenous tiger with a bucket of chicken feed.

'Sorry! Sorry! Sorry!' sobbed Cissy. 'How was I to know? We're teetotal in our house!'

Climbing back over the barricade of buckled grilles and cash-boxes, telegraphic machinery and ink-bloody blotters, they finally reached the back doors of the bank and stumbled out into the street. The keys sent to the Junkers, to ease their entry, still hung from the keyhole. Kookie pocketed them for evidence, but had to let go one corner of the cloak to do it, and Billy rolled over.

'H'ven sakes, Kooks! My arms are dropping out!'

On the other side of the road stood row upon row of plank-wood huts, each no bigger than a chuck wagon and not one with a light burning in its window, (not one with even a window). These were the comfortless homes to which the Darkville miners returned after a day's labour in the mines. Beyond them, a pit-head wheel caught the rising moon in its spokes. It peered at Cissy and Kookie, like a condemned face at a prison window.

'Not much further, Billy,' said Cissy. 'Nearly there.'

'Unfortunately,' said Everett Crew, 'the good people of Florence had never seen theatre before and mistook my play-acting for the genuine article. A man in the back row took out his gun and . . .'

'Come to the present.'

Jack Shakespeare had left his hotel room and appeared now in the street, in leather riding coat and Confederate-style cavalry hat. He carried a shotgun over his arm. 'Come to the part about robbing my bank,' he said.

Everett took some time to focus on the Owner of Darkville: he had been concentrating so intently on his speech. Now a host of questions came clamouring back into his head. What would become of the children still hidden in the theatre? What could he do to ensure the women's safety? He found no answers to his questions. 'The bank? Ah! There we enter the realms of fiction!' he answered. 'We may have briefly shared a train with the robbers, but does that mean we knew them? No! No more than it means I am related to the guard or married to the engine driver!'

A section of the crowd, calmer now, had warmed to Crew. They were half inclined to believe him, disinclined to hang him.

But Jack Shakespeare preferred his workers violent and unthinking. Let them once stoop to Rope Law and they would be in his power ever after. 'I made enquiries. Seems every place these *actors* have been, the bank's been raided.' There was a gasp from the crowd.

'No!' said Loucien.

'That's a lie!' said Cyril Crew.

'Hang them,' said the Owner. 'Just git on and do it.'

'Stop!'

The crowd, startled by the unfamiliar sight of two children in a childless town, parted to let Cissy and Kookie through. They were waddling, bandy-legged under the weight of a bundle of cloth. Grubby, singed, and weary to the point of exhaustion, they nonetheless laid their load down gently. The big dray horse lowered its head to sniff at the musty cloak with its cabalistic signs, its spattering of sealing wax, ink, and brick dust.

'Cissy—Kookie—why didn't you just stay put?' Loucien asked in horror.

'No, no! It's all right! This is Billy! He can tell them! He's a witness!' Cissy gasped for breath.

Jack Shakespeare eased the shotgun from the crook of his arm and snapped it straight.

'He can tell you the Bright Lights weren't part of it!' Kookie urged the crowd, as Cissy gently folded back the cloak.

The cents that had peppered Billy Junker when the safe blew glimmered in the gaslight, almost as if he were wearing the chain mail of a knight.

'Tell them, Billy!' said Kookie, dancing from foot to foot. 'Tell them how we didn't have anything to do with it! Tell them how there wasn't anything there. How it was already gone!'

The Owner wrapped his finger around the trigger of the shotgun.

But Billy Junker had forgotten all about the excitements of the afternoon: his high hope of riches, his surprise at the size of the explosion, his disappointment at finding the safe empty. In fact he had forgotten all the disappointments of his young life. His face was serene. Somewhere between the darkness of the under-stage and the moonlit town square, he had forgotten everything he ever knew.

Even how to breathe.

So there it was in front of their very eyes—the proof: one of the bank robbers in the care of two child actors. The bank keys in Kookie's hand were like an admission of guilt. They dangled from his upraised finger like a company of hanged men.

'Billy could've told you!' said Cissy to a wall of aggressive faces. 'Nobody took your money because there wasn't any . . .'

Jack Shakespeare fired his shotgun to obliterate Cissy's words. The noise startled the dray horse and sent it trampling backwards through the crowd, unleashing confusion and anger. The men holding the hanging rope did not need telling their duty. They snatched it tight and heaved.

'*NO!*' cried Cissy.

'*NO!*' cried Millie and clapped her hands over the children's eyes.

'*NO!*' cried Egil and jumped to try and intercept the rope above Crew's head.

'*STOP!*' cried Cyril Crew, and launched himself at the men pulling on the rope.

Only Loucien, her eyes transfixed by her beloved husband's face, saw him glance upwards—as a man does who sees Heaven open and angels beckon. She followed his gaze and, for a split second, could not make sense of what she was seeing.

For the lynch mob seemed not to be hauling Crew up to his death, but hauling the hotel down to its knees.

The balcony through which the rope was threaded was falling—and not just the balcony but the whole hotel.

'*LOOK OUT!*' shouted Everett, whisking the noose from around his throat. Then, reaching down to snatch the children's hands, he dragged them clear off the ground—up against the horse's withers—and drove the animal forwards with yells and kicks and slaps and every encouragement that was ever given a horse to move.

No one responds quicker to a shout of warning than a bunch of miners. They heard and they ran. But as they ran they looked back over their shoulders and barely believed their eyes; for they saw the Slaked Snake Saloon smash like a single glass of golden beer, the Imperial Shakespeare Theatre stagger like a drunk, the Ritz Dance Hall dancing. The Calliope Palais had disappeared completely from sight.

Only the solitary figure of Jack Shakespeare was left staring dully at the shotgun in his hands, believing he had shot his own hotel and felled it to its knees. The Plaza Hotel was sinking—not collapsing but sinking into the ground! Its windows passed him by like an elevator on its way down to Hell. The ground was opening like a giant mouth, to swallow the entire lavish splendour of the town square.

And it roared as it fed.

Chapter Six
Company

When Jack Shakespeare decided to rob his own bank, he should never have entrusted the job to enthusiastic amateurs. What with the Junkers' inexperience and Shakespeare's extra wrap of dynamite, the explosion had done more than blow the door from the safe, kill Billy, and demolish half the bank. It had managed to undermine the Owner's world.

The mines of Darkville had once been open-cast quarries scarring the ugly landscape. But new, greedier shafts had then been sunk. Like legs stretched out beneath a table, they struck downwards at an angle, groping under the town for the ore lying hidden there. A honeycomb of shafts now riddled the earth beneath Darkville.

'*Cave in! Cave in!*' The cry was taken up by the running miners, like a battle-cry. Underground shafts had been weakened by the blast, and now they were collapsing, like a dead man's arteries. The subsidence seemed to go on for hours, and yet within a minute the town square had come to rest, like a camel settling to its haunches. Here and there deep fissures had opened up, but most of the garish glamour of the square was still visible, in the bottom of a smoking bowl resembling the crater of a volcano. Fire licked the fractured rooftops, and the air was full of smoke and dust and slivers of burning timber.

The miners who had thrown themselves face-down were dredged with this 'fall-out' of dirt, only visible when they stirred and began to drag themselves to their feet. The white dray horse being led around the perimeter of the crater became first dappled, then blackened, as did the shirt of the man leading it.

'Loucien? Loucien Crew!' he called, and the children riding one behind the other on the big horse called too. *'Miss Loucien! Where are you?'*

The Owner of the town stood just as before, on the brink of the cave-in, pointing at the roof of the hotel and bleating through a throatful of dust, 'Money! My money!'

'Must be where he has the loot from the bank,' said Kookie. Being only eleven years old, he was able to think in more than one direction at once.

Being forty, Crew could not. *'Loucien! Where are you, sweetheart?'*

'Think. All those men's money just swallowed up in the ground,' said Kookie.

'Ah, come on, Loucien! Please!'

'Someone needs to get it back for 'em.'

'Shsh, Kookie. Hush up,' hissed Cissy into the nape of his neck. 'He's got other things on his mind. And what's money alongside Miss Loucien?'

The dust fell so thickly it was barely possible to see one yard ahead. *'Loucien, honey!'* called Crew, but the air was full of people shouting the names of friends and brothers and workmates.

'Hold thy peace! I prithee hold thy peace!' Cissy began to sing—a wavering, reedy jumble of half-hit notes.

Crew turned and looked at her, uncomprehending for a moment. Then he joined in. The song, hitting a different frequency, carried better than shouts did: *'Hold thy peace! I prithee hold thy peace!'*

Through the murk came answering refrains, and one by one the Bright Lights—Revere, Finn, Millie, Cyril—converged on one another, their timing ragged but their handshakes eager and relieved. Cissy listened and listened for the sound of Miss Loucien's voice. Everett, too, had his hands cupped behind his ears. But the miners had begun to join in the singing now, finding the tune familiar without remembering why. The monotonous fugue chased itself round the rim of the crater:

'Hold thy peace! I prithee hold thy . . . Hold thy peace! I prithee hold thy . . . Hold thy peace! I prithee . . .'

The ground rumbled and growled out a bass line.

Men were scrambling down towards the splintery ruins of their puny huts, several of which had been toppled into the pit as if led astray by the grander buildings. They were struggling to retrieve their few pitiful possessions, risking their lives on the unstable slopes for the sake of a coffee pot, a chequer board, a suitcase . . . At any moment the subsidence might begin again.

Jack Shakespeare also yearned after his lost

belongings, but could not persuade his henchmen to venture down into the crater on his behalf. Thinking him ruined by the bank robbery, they simply turned their backs on him, mounted up, and rode away in search of a different tyrant to serve. Shakespeare did not try to stop them. He had not let them in on his little scheme to steal the town's money (some of it was theirs), and he dared not tell them now. Nor did he dare to climb down himself. The hotel's chimneys protruded like the shoots of a potato buried in the ground. At any moment the pressure of the soil might crush the hotel flatter than a billboard. In his distress, he had no idea that he was actually cursing under his breath: ' . . . *all that money . . . all that d****d money . . . all that **** . . .* '

'I'll go,' said a voice.

Shakespeare looked down at the boy who had appeared at his side as red-haired and scrawny as a Rhode Island chicken.

'I'll go over there. At a price. How much you paying?'

'Ten dollars.'

'Fifty.'

'Fifty, then, damn you,' said the Owner. 'I just want two satchels. They're hanging behind my bedroom door. Two leather satchels. You got that?'

It was not until the boy had started down the landslip that Shakespeare noticed the rope around his waist. It was of whitish hemp, and the knot fastening it behind his waist was the kind used in a noose. Holding the end of this lifeline were the men of the Bright Lights Theatre Company.

The dirt beneath Kookie's feet rippled and trickled

and ran. It was like trying to walk down a waterfall. Little avalanches set off, piling up yet more soil around the sunken buildings, burying them deeper and deeper. Windows cracked under the weight of earth, then broke, and swallowed the soil through their broken panes. At any moment another of the unstable tunnels under the town might collapse and allow more huts to crumble, more buildings to plunge. Whenever he came to a halt, Kookie had to spread his weight, or the loose soil tried to swallow him like quicksand. He was glad when he reached the roof of the hotel; it at least gave the illusion of a solid platform.

Tiles crackled under him. He crawled on hands and knees towards the only skylight, but ran out of rope before he got there, and had to slip out of the noose to crawl the last few feet without a safety line. Even so, his friends were still so close that he could hear Millie's voice saying, 'We shouldn'ta let him, Cyril. He's not ours to let,' and Cyril answering, 'He's the only one small enough and light enough.'

'Nothing to it!' Kookie called to them, with tinny bravado. 'Done worse than this any Tuesday in the year!'

Then he was through the skylight and inside the Plaza Hotel, dropping down on to a big goosefeather bed.

Smoke nettled the back of his throat. Somewhere, the gas-lamps had spilled their fire. Curtains were ablaze, rugs were charring. He hoped the fire had not reached Shakespeare's bedroom.

The skylight let in moonlight, but as soon as Kookie stepped into the corridor, he was in total darkness. *This is how dark it would be to be dead and buried.* He had to grope his way along the landing wall and down the stairs . . . 'Ah!'

His feeling foot found no stair. The twisting of the building had broken the stairs' spine. But the banister seemed to be intact. He climbed astride it and let himself slide—slowly, slowly—down to the floor below. Now he had to find the Owner's suite of rooms, the right bags behind the right door.

What a waste! Never in his life had Kookie Warboys set foot inside a classy hotel, and here he was among goosefeather mattresses and brass ashtrays and those three-fold mirrors that let you see the back of your own head. And he could enjoy none of it! He could see *nothing*. ' . . . Oh!'

Something woolly had got him by the feet! But it was only a bedside rug. The building around him groaned and creaked, tons of earth pressing on it from every side, squeezing it to death.

Kookie opened a door, stepped round it—and something punched him in the side of the head. As he recoiled, something else sandbagged him from behind. Then his head was being socked: right, left; right, left. In pure self defence, Kookie raised his hands—and felt the straps of two leather satchels. Suddenly he realized that he could see. The four sides of a square, like the red fringe of a carpet, ruffled and rippled, outlining the floor. Fire must be licking at the ceiling of the room below, breaking through where wall met floor! He looped the straps across his body. Each bag seemed to weigh as much as a millstone—and his knees bent under the strain. How would he ever climb back out through the roof, burdened down like this? In the dark, he collided with the door.

Kookie wormed his way up the slippery banister like Satan heading for the Garden of Eden, the buckles of the satchels blipping out a tune on the wrought-iron railings. He was sweating so much with fear that he could not judge whether the fire below him was getting fiercer. His eyes struggled almost clean out of his head trying to catch the gleam of moonlight. The first bedroom he came to held none at all. *The hotel has slipped down underground!* No. Wrong room. He felt his way next door.

And there was the skylight—the high, inaccessible skylight. Even standing on the bed, ankle-deep in softness, the two heavy bags cutting into his shoulders, he knew he had no means of climbing those last twelve feet of empty air. He would go down with the Plaza Hotel, like a sailor in a foundering ship, anchored underground with thousands of stolen dollar bills.

'*Hey, Kooks! Grab hold!*' A length of hangman's rope blipped him on the neck. 'Is it real ritzy down there?' called Cissy.

Kookie shrugged off the bags and tied one on to the rope. 'Seen better,' he said. A few minutes later, as he struggled through the little skylight and joined her on the roof, he said, 'Don't be took in; you can't see the back of your head in them three-bit looking glasses.'

He was interrupted then by a surge of cheering that grew to a racketing roar. On the spot where he had left his friends holding the rope's end, there was now a huge crowd of cheering miners.

The truth had finally penetrated Darkville. Now the grateful town greeted Kookie and Cissy with yelps and

54

whoops and cheers that set the loose soil a-slither and drowned out the noise of the Calliope Palais being slowly pulverized to matchwood underground.

Jack Shakespeare was nowhere to be seen. Just as he had knocked the heart out of his 'company men', he had managed to knock the heart out of his empire and lose his own loot in the process. Nothing remained but to creep away from the miners' wrath, with the taste of dirt in his mouth.

And all of a sudden, there, in his place, was Loucien Crew—emerging from the dust like Boudicca from the smoking ruins of Colchester; like Cleopatra sailing out of battle. In one hand was her husband's hat, while from the other, like a chain of paper dollies cut from newspaper, trailed a string of young women in bodice and bloomers—the rare and distinctive ladies of Darkville.

'*Oh, Miss Loucien, you're alive!*' cried Cissy, wriggling her waist out of the rope's noose to run and hug her teacher.

Loucien Crew placed the hat on Cissy's head, then ran her eyes over the full cast of the Bright Lights Theatre Company: Curly—Millie—Cyril—Revere—Egil—Finn—the Two Descending Spirits. And Everett.

'Some show stopper,' she said wryly.

But Crew simply took the hat Cissy brought him and, resting it low on his brow, turned his back for a long moment and wiped the dirt from his face with the sleeve of his shirt.

*　*　*

Just before dawn came up, Kookie played his mouth organ, and Loucien sang—a song attuned to the hardships of the Darkville men.

A kind of plaintive sweetness pierced the leathery hearts of the miners and set them wondering whether life could and should be brighter than theirs had so far been. Cissy had told them they should quit Darkville for Oklahoma where there were no company towns and a man's soul was his own. But the men of Darkville were content. Their savings had been restored to them. Some would go home to their neglected families with what they had mustered. Some would stay, for the town (such as it was) belonged to them now; in future they would not be the serfs of any tyrannical overlord.

Kookie played and Loucien sang. And in the darkness, there was a silver tinkle of coins being thrown —not cents thrown in malice, as before, but dollars thrown in appreciation—a small show of silver to help the Bright Lights on their way. The sunlight rose on a small pile of coins about the size of a cowpat. Those coins spoke the words the miners could not say, never having benefited from the vocabulary of the poets or the mind-expanding riches of drama.

By the time their trains pulled out of Darkville Station—Cissy and Kookie bound for Olive, Oklahoma, the Bright Lights for the sultry south—almost all the fires were out. Only a little pall of ash-blond smoke hung high in the sky over the sunken crater: the ghost of Billy Junker, perhaps, on his way up to the bright lights of Heaven.

Read more about Cissy, Kookie and Miss Loucien in…

STOP THE TRAIN

Highly Commended for the Carnegie Medal
Winner of the Smarties Bronze Award

'the work of a great writer …
I cannot recommend it strongly enough'
Times Educational Supplement

'an excellent, unpredictable and engrossing novel
from a genuine master of the imagination'
Independent

'a triumph … unforgettable' *The Sunday Times*

£4.99 paperback 0 19 275266 9

Other fantastic books by Geraldine McCaughrean

0 19 275091 7   £4.99

0 19 271884 3   £6.99
Shortlisted for the Carnegie Medal

0 19 275290 1   £4.99
Winner of the Whitbread
Children's Novel Award

0 19 271876 2   £6.99
Winner of the Nestlé
Smarties Bronze Award

0 19 275157 3   £4.99
Winner of the Blue Peter
'Best Book to Keep Forever' Award
Winner of the Nestlé
Smarties Bronze Award
Shortlisted for the Carnegie Medal

0 19 275203 0   £4.99
Winner of the Carnegie Medal
Winner of the Guardian
Children's Fiction Award